The Frightened Puppy

Other titles by Holly Webb

Lost in the Snow	The Kidnapped Kitten
Alfie all Alone	The Scruffy Puppy
Lost in the Storm	The Brave Kitten
Sam the Stolen Puppy	The Forgotten Puppy
Max the Missing Puppy	The Secret Kitten
Sky the Unwanted Kitten	A Home for Molly
Timmy in Trouble	Sammy the Shy Kitten
Ginger the Stray Kitten	The Seaside Puppy
Harry the Homeless Puppy	The Curious Kitten
Buttons the Runaway Puppy	Monty the Sad Puppy
Alone in the Night	The Homeless Kitten
Ellie the Homesick Puppy	A Kitten Called Tiger
Jess the Lonely Puppy	The Unwanted Puppy
Misty the Abandoned Kitten	The Rescued Kitten
Oscar's Lonely Christmas	The Shelter Puppy
Lucy the Poorly Puppy	The Perfect Kitten
Smudge the Stolen Kitten	The Puppy Who Couldn't Sleep
The Rescued Puppy	The Loneliest Kitten
The Kitten Nobody Wanted	The Mystery Kitten
The Lost Puppy	The Story Puppy
The Frightened Kitten	The Kitten Next Door
The Secret Puppy	The Puppy Who Ran Away
The Abandoned Puppy	Nadia and the Forever Kitten
The Missing Kitten	A Puppy's First Christmas
The Puppy who was Left Behind	The Homesick Kitten

The Frightened Puppy

Holly Webb
Illustrated by Sophy Williams

LITTLE TIGER

LONDON

For Sarah and Buddy

STRIPES PUBLISHING LIMITED
An imprint of the Little Tiger Group
1 Coda Studios, 189 Munster Road, London SW6 6AW

Imported into the EEA by Penguin Random House Ireland,
Morrison Chambers, 32 Nassau Street, Dublin D02 YH68

A paperback original
First published in Great Britain in 2022

Text copyright © Holly Webb, 2022
Illustrations copyright © Sophy Williams, 2022
Author photograph © Charlotte Knee Photography

ISBN: 978-1-78895-388-7

A CIP catalogue record for this book is available from the British Library.

Printed and bound in the UK.

Chapter One

Avery peered excitedly out of the window as Mum parked the car at the side of their holiday cottage. "I can see the river!"

Avery's older brother, Noah, leaned over her shoulder to look too. "Wow. It really is just at the bottom of the garden!"

"Let's go and take a quick look at it

before we unpack," Mum suggested.

Dad undid his seat belt and got out of the car, stretching and sighing after their long drive. "Come on then. This place is amazing…"

The cottage garden was enormous – nothing like their garden back at home. It seemed to stretch out forever, and there was a field on one side and a patch of woodland on the other. There was just a little low fence with a gate at the end – and then the river. The water looked dark and greenish, and the banks were full of reeds and rushes and ferns. There were tiny plops and splashes here and there which made Avery think of fish – maybe even otters!

"Oh goodness, it looks deep," Mum

murmured. "Avery, I don't want you out here by the river on your own – it's not safe."

"Mum!" Avery turned an outraged look on her. "I'm not a baby – I'm nine! I'm not going to fall in the river!"

"Don't worry, Avery," Dad said soothingly. "We're going to be too busy for anyone to go falling in rivers. Your mum has booked for us to go mountain biking in the hills tomorrow, remember! And we've got lots of other fun trips planned too."

"But today's just for settling in," Mum said. "Why don't we go and make a start on unpacking, then we can bring those sandwiches I made this morning out here? We can put a rug down and have a picnic by the river."

"Yes!" Avery nodded eagerly. She'd been for walks by the river that ran through their town, and she loved feeding the ducks and looking at the huge swans, but that river was wide and slow. It ran between concrete paths and tall buildings for most of its way, and it wasn't nearly as interesting as this wild river at the bottom of the garden. Further up, Avery could see trees leaning over and trailing in the water. She imagined that out on the river it would be like sailing through a tunnel of green.

Still – there was the cottage to explore too. "Let's go and look at the bedrooms," Avery suggested, starting to race back up the garden. If she got there first, she could choose the nicest room...

The cottage was quite small but it had an attic bedroom tucked away at the top, which Avery loved – if she leaned out of the tiny window in the thatched roof she could just see the river through the trees. She could hear birds twittering and rustling in the thatch, and the air smelled sweet from all the flowers in the garden. She hadn't been that excited when Mum and Dad had told them they were going on holiday to a cottage in the country for two whole weeks. She'd wanted to go somewhere hot, or maybe a theme park, but now she was so glad they'd come.

She quickly put her clothes in the chest of drawers by her bed and then hurried downstairs to have a good look at the other rooms. There was an open fireplace in the living room, with a pile of wood next to it. Perhaps if there was a cold wet day they could have a fire? Maybe even toast marshmallows?

"Is it lunchtime yet?" Avery asked Mum hopefully as she went into the kitchen. "Can we go down to the river?"

Mum laughed and handed Avery a cool bag that she'd brought from home. "Here you go. Take that out, and I'll bring the rug and some drinks." She went to the door and called up the stairs for Noah and Dad while Avery went out into the sunny garden. Mum and the others were following her, of course, but she had a moment or two where it was just her, standing by the river, listening to the water moving over the stones.

Then Noah came stomping noisily down the garden with his arms full of cushions. "Dad found these in a box outside," he explained, spilling them on to the grass.

"Is your room nice?" Avery asked him and Noah shrugged.

"It's OK. No WiFi here, though." He slumped down against the cushions and pulled his phone out of his pocket as Mum and Dad arrived with the rug and a tray of drinks.

Mum passed around the rolls – she had made everyone's favourites. Avery's was just plain butter because that meant she could put her crisps inside. She wasn't allowed to do that for packed lunches at school, so it felt like a holiday treat. She was crunching and licking crumbs off her lips and watching the river when she heard a new sound echoing above the birdsong – a splashing sound, and voices.

"Oh, is it a boat?" Dad said, sitting up to look.

Even Noah put down his phone for a minute to see what was happening as round the bend of the river came two long, open canoes. A family with four children was paddling along and they waved at Avery and the others on the bank. Avery waved back, a bit shyly – and then she realized that in the front of the first canoe was a beautiful chocolate Labrador.

"Look at the dog!" Avery whispered, nudging Dad, and Dad laughed.

"He's having the time of his life! Lucky dog, he doesn't have to paddle."

"He's got a life jacket on," Noah pointed out. "Maybe he likes jumping in."

Just as Noah said it, the chocolate Lab seemed to spot them and their picnic for the first time. He stood up, eyeing the cake that Mum had just started slicing, and then flung himself into the water.

"Freddy! Get back here!"

"NO!"

"Freddy, don't you dare!"

The whole family started shouting at once, but Avery watched delightedly as Freddy paddled across to the bank and scrambled out on to the muddy, pebbly edge of the river. He gave himself a huge shake and trotted hopefully up to the rug.

"Er, I don't think you're supposed to be doing this," Dad told him, smiling. He put out a hand and let Freddy sniff him and lick his fingers. He was still looking at the cake, though.

The oldest boy, who'd been sitting just behind Freddy in the canoe, was now splashing hurriedly through the river, looking apologetic. The water only came up to his knees – Avery hadn't realized it was so shallow. That was good – maybe Mum wouldn't be so worried about her being down by the river now.

"Freddy, come here!" The boy grabbed hold of the dog's life jacket and pulled him back gently. "I'm really sorry, I should have caught him before he jumped. He didn't eat anything, did he?"

"No, don't worry." Mum was laughing. "He was hoping for cake, I think. He's lovely."

"He's a greedy monster. Sorry to have disturbed you."

"Can I stroke him?" Avery asked hopefully. She loved dogs and she'd always thought Labradors were gorgeous – they were so clever too. She was a bit worried that the boy would say no, but he smiled at her.

"Sure. He's really friendly. He likes his ears being rubbed."

Avery reached out and stroked Freddy's ears. He stuck his nose up in the air and half closed his eyes, like it was the best thing that had ever happened.

"You're gorgeous," Avery whispered to him. She could just imagine how fun it would be to have a dog like Freddy with them on holiday. They could go exploring up the riverbank together – maybe even go swimming…

"Thanks for not minding him getting in the way. We should get back. Bye!" The boy coaxed Freddy back into the water and over to the canoe. Then he had to stand in the middle of the river, trying to heave a wriggly, wet Labrador into the canoe while all his family shouted advice. Avery had to press her hand over her mouth to stop herself laughing out loud when he kicked water all over the boy.

Eventually the family paddled on, looking a bit damp and red-faced, leaving Avery and her family giggling on the bank.

"I feel like we should have given that poor boy some cake, let alone the dog," Mum said.

"I'd love a dog like that," Avery said enviously.

"What, one that raids picnics?" Noah said.

"No! A Labrador! He was so handsome!"

"Yeah, actually, he was a really nice dog," Noah said, agreeing with her for once. "Friendly too."

Mum shook her head. "He was beautiful but think of all the looking after. A big dog like that needs loads of walking. You wouldn't want to get up early every day to walk a dog before school, would you?"

Avery frowned. Actually, that

sounded fun. She always woke up early and read a book or drew before it was time to get up. She'd quite like to go for a walk instead. But Noah shuddered. He hated getting up – he was always arguing with Mum about it.

"Canoeing looked fun," Dad said, gazing thoughtfully at the river. "Did you see, those canoes said the name of a hire place on them? We could try that, later on in the week."

Mum and Dad and Noah started talking about the different activities they had planned but Avery didn't join in. She was remembering how soft Freddy's ears had been, and wishing she could have stroked him for longer.

Chapter Two

Everyone was exhausted after their mountain biking trip, so they spent the next day lazing around in the garden to let their legs recover. But on the fourth day of the holiday, they went for a trip on the river.

Unfortunately, the canoe hire place had already booked out all the big canoes – but they did have lots of one-person kayaks, and Dad arranged a teaching session so they'd all know what they were doing before they went out on the water. They happened to see the family with Freddy the Labrador there too. They had obviously enjoyed themselves so much that they were going out again. Avery got to make a fuss of Freddy and he was so delighted that she was sure he must remember her – or maybe he just remembered the cake…

Being on the water was even more exciting than Avery had hoped. She felt like an explorer as they wound around the bends of the river. Because the kayaks moved so quietly – even when Noah kept splashing with his paddle – they got much closer to the birds along the riverbank than they would have done walking. Dad pointed out a heron perched on a fallen log at the side of the river and for a moment or two Avery thought it was a statue it was so still. Then it realized they were getting near and leaped into the air, beating its huge wings and trailing long, spindly legs as it flapped away.

Avery was a bit behind Mum and Dad and Noah, imagining herself up a wild, unexplored river, when she caught sight of something moving on the bank. She stilled her paddle, thinking maybe it was a rabbit. She nearly called for the others, sure that they'd want to see – but she didn't want to scare the little creature away. She sat quietly watching instead.

It wasn't a rabbit. There among the reeds at the edge of the river was a small brown dog. A puppy. Avery felt herself smiling – the puppy was so sweet, with big, dark round eyes and a whiskery face. It was really tiny too, Avery thought. Actually, she was surprised that it was old enough to be out on a walk without its lead on. What if it decided to jump in the river like Freddy? She looked along the riverbank, wondering who the puppy belonged to. The little brown dog was gazing back at her and Avery was sure she saw it wag its tail, just a tiny bit.

As quietly as she could, Avery paddled closer to the bank. The puppy was still watching her, its ears pricked. Avery was sure it was friendly – it looked so curious. She had the sudden thought that the puppy would fit perfectly on her lap inside the well of the canoe – but that was silly…

"Hello!" she whispered, and the puppy edged further forwards. "Oh, don't get too near the edge," she added quickly.

"Avery, come on!" There was a

sudden shout from down the river
and she jumped, almost dropping her
paddle. It clattered on to the top of the
kayak and the puppy seemed to jump
too. It scooted away under the trees,
leaving Avery watching after it sadly.

"Avery, are you all right?" That was
Mum, sounding worried, and Avery
sighed, digging her paddle hard into
the water to catch up.

"I'm OK. I'm coming," she called.

"What were you doing?" Mum
asked as she caught up with the
others. Avery was about to tell her
about the puppy but somehow the
words stuck in her throat. It was her
secret. If she told Mum and Dad and
Noah, some of the specialness of that
moment would be gone.

"I thought I saw a rabbit," she explained, shrugging a little. "Sorry!"

"OK. Let's try and stay together."

Avery nodded and they paddled on, but she was hardly noticing the river now. She just kept thinking about that little dog and the tiny wag of its tail.

The puppy huddled underneath the bramble bush, listening to the voices floating past. They sounded – she didn't quite know what they sounded like. Different to the voices she knew, which were loud and sometimes angry. These voices made her want to wriggle out from her hiding place, so she could see who they belonged to. But she didn't quite dare. She just listened, until the voices and the splashing had moved on. Then she squeezed out underneath the prickly stems and padded to the water's edge.

She'd thought that the people had all gone – she'd wanted to peer after them, to see them without them seeing her – but one of them was still there. A girl. She was looking curiously at the puppy and there was something about her, something friendly and gentle.

"Hello!" Her voice was very soft, but she sounded excited and the puppy felt her tail twitch, just a little. She crept forwards, closer to the water.

The girl had started speaking again, when there came a shout from further down the river and then a strange, loud, clattering noise as the girl dropped something. The puppy tensed up all over. She knew about shouting and loud noises – she knew to stay away.

It was time to go.

The puppy whisked round and darted back under the bramble bushes, where she was hidden and safe. She stayed crouched there, listening carefully, until she was sure she'd heard the girl paddle away.

After a while, the puppy crept back to the edge of the river, watching. The riverbank was very quiet now and even more empty than it had seemed before. She hadn't seen any people for a while. She'd hoped the girl might have some food to give her. She hadn't had anything to eat, not for such a long time, and she was so hungry.

The puppy looked wearily along the river, wondering what to do. Everything felt so strange and wrong. Only a couple of days ago, she'd been curled up next to her mother, half snoozing after a feed, thinking that soon there would be a bowl of biscuits to eat too. Instead, she'd been snatched up and stuffed into a box and shut away in the dark. She'd crouched there trembling, listening to her mother whining and yapping frantically. She could hear her clawing and scrabbling at the man holding the box until he shouted at her, and inside the box the puppy had flinched and frozen.

She'd been too bewildered to understand what was happening – the strange, sickening lurching, and the way the box seemed to shudder and shake. Then someone had picked the box up again and she'd felt herself be carried for a while. After that, nothing. The box was on the ground somewhere quiet and that was all. She could hear a few birds twittering but all the sounds were muffled by the box.

The puppy had waited for a long while. She waited for someone to come back and fetch her. For her mother to find her and curl up next to her and lick her ears. She didn't understand what was happening and why she was all alone. At last, she shoved and clawed and managed to tip the box over and wriggle out between the loose flaps at the top. She'd found herself on the riverbank, completely abandoned. She'd whined sadly, frightened by the quiet and the loneliness and the swiftly flowing water. It was all so strange. She had been here ever since, huddled under the brambles, listening to the wild creatures snuffle and rustle as they padded by. She hadn't dared to explore much further than the edge of the bank.

Now she whined again, calling for someone to curl up next to her so she felt warm and safe and loved, but no one came.

Chapter Three

"Can we go kayaking again today?" Avery suggested the next morning. Mum and Dad were drinking coffee and eating toast, and they looked happy and holiday-ish. It seemed a good time to ask.

Mum looked surprised. "You really want to? It was quite hard work…"

"Didn't you like it?" Avery said, feeling

disappointed. She'd hoped they might be able to go exploring along the river again and she would see that little brown dog. Avery had been thinking about it ever since – or her. She couldn't help thinking that the puppy was a girl, she didn't know why. The puppy had seemed so nervous and she'd been all on her own. What if there was something wrong? Avery had thought she was just out on a walk and a bit far from her owner, or maybe she'd slipped out of her garden. But perhaps she was lost?

"It was fun for a day," Mum explained. "But, well, I just felt damp all the time! There was a little puddle of water in the bottom of that kayak…"

Dad nodded. "I know what you mean. It was great getting to see the banks

of the river from the water, though –
everything looked so different."

"Wouldn't you like to?" Avery asked
Noah hopefully. He'd definitely enjoyed
the kayaking, even if he had moaned
about his phone getting wet.

Noah shrugged, not bothering to look
up from his phone.

"What about a walk?" Mum
suggested. "There's that old water mill a
couple of miles down the river, we could
walk there, it's on our side of the bank.
We could take a picnic to eat by the
river and then get ice creams at the café
afterwards." She reached over to the
little stand of leaflets that the cottage
owners had put on the kitchen counter,
about different places to visit. "Here.
Doesn't it look nice?"

Avery nodded eagerly. The water mill did look interesting, with a huge wheel to turn the machinery, but more importantly they'd be walking along the side of the river exactly where they'd kayaked yesterday. Perhaps the little dog would still be around. Or if she wasn't, that was a good thing too, wasn't it? It would mean she hadn't been lost after all.

Avery wasn't really sure what she was hoping for.

Avery only nibbled at her sandwich. It was just bread and butter – she hadn't bothered to put the crisps in today. She didn't feel like it. They'd walked all the way to the mill and she hadn't seen the puppy. Not even a hint of brown fur, not anywhere.

Avery took another slow bite. Why was she feeling so disappointed? The puppy had gone home with her owner – that was all. She shouldn't have expected anything else.

"Aren't you hungry, sweetheart?" Dad asked. "No crisps?"

Avery shrugged. "Can I eat them later? I just don't feel like them right now. I ate the other half of the sandwich."

"I suppose so," Mum said. "But have some fruit. Especially if you want an ice cream." She handed Avery a banana and Avery nodded, tucking the sandwich and the crisps away in her backpack with her waterproof. She tried to look excited about the ice cream – she didn't want to explain to Mum and Dad why she was feeling sad, especially as she didn't really know the answer herself. There had been something so special about that moment the day before, when the puppy started to creep towards her. She had wanted it to last longer. And today

she'd had this strange, certain feeling
that she would see the puppy again. It
was hard to admit that she must have
imagined it.

Avery shook herself crossly and
swallowed a lump of banana. She was
just being silly.

They ate the ice creams on the walk
back to the cottage. Avery got half
toffee caramel and half lemon, and
Noah said that was disgusting, but his
was half strawberry and half peanut
butter, so he couldn't talk. Avery was
wandering along behind the others,
trying to get the last bits of ice cream
before her cone completely fell apart,
when she saw the puppy again.

It was such a surprise that she
actually dropped her ice cream cone.

Avery saw the little brown dog's eyes snap to it at once – clearly she was starving and she wanted to gobble it up. But she didn't step out of the clump of reedy grass where she was half hidden. She didn't dare. Her ears were flattened back and her eyes were round and wide. She was shaking, Avery could see it.

"Hey…" Avery whispered. "It's OK. You can eat it. Are you hungry?" She backed up the path a little, leaving space for the puppy to get to the ice cream cone without having to come too close. Then she crouched down – she wasn't quite sure why. She wanted to make herself look small too, small and not scary. The tiny dog seemed so frightened.

Avery sat quietly for a moment, hoping and hoping that Dad wouldn't call for her again and send the puppy running like he had the day before. At last the puppy edged out of the grass clump and padded cautiously towards Avery and the ice cream. She lowered her head and started to bolt down the remains of the cone – but she kept stopping to make sure Avery wasn't coming any nearer. Avery wondered why she was so afraid.

"Is that nice?" she whispered. "Oh! I've got more, I forgot. Half a sandwich and a packet of crisps. They're cheese and onion, is that OK?" Then she giggled to herself. The puppy didn't look as if she cared what flavour the crisps were. She'd probably eat anything.

Very slowly, Avery eased her backpack off her shoulders, trying to do it without frightening the little dog away. "It's all right," she murmured gently when she saw the puppy freeze. "I'm getting you more. Here, look…" She brought out the foil-wrapped sandwich and peeled back the covering, showing the bread to the puppy. "Here you go." She reached out slowly and laid the sandwich between them.

The puppy watched suspiciously for a moment and then grabbed the corner of the sandwich in her teeth and pulled it away from Avery, before she began to wolf it down.

"You really are hungry," Avery said, reaching into her backpack for the crisps. "I hope these are OK for dogs. My friend Iris said her cat loves cheese and onion crisps..." She pulled the packet open and spilled the crisps on to the ground, then she glanced up at the path ahead – there was no sign of Mum and Dad and Noah. "Oh wow, I've got to go – they'll be wondering where I am."

She stood up carefully and the puppy stopped eating crisps to watch her go. "You'd better get back home too, puppy." Avery frowned worriedly. "But whoever you belong to can't be feeding you enough. I'm not sure they're very nice owners." She looked rather guiltily at the pile of crisps. It probably wasn't a good thing to feed someone else's dog, even if you did think it wasn't being properly looked after. Avery's Auntie Meg had got really cross when someone down

the street started feeding her cat
Snowball. She'd said it felt as if her
neighbours were trying to tempt him
away, almost as if they wanted to steal
him. Avery remembered Mum on the
phone to Auntie Meg, saying that it
was a terrible thing to do…

But the puppy had looked so
hungry, and so scared. Avery couldn't
not help her…

She whispered goodbye to the
puppy and then hurried down the
path to catch up with Mum and Dad
and Noah. She kept looking back
every moment or two, to see if the
little dog was following her. If she
was, did that mean she was lost? Or
was it just that she liked snacks and
Avery had fed her?

Maybe I shouldn't have given her the sandwich and the crisps, Avery thought to herself. *Though the ice cream was an accident...*

But there was so sign of a little brown puppy hurrying after her. Perhaps she'd gone home to her owner after all.

Further back along the path, too far back for Avery to spot her, the puppy was scurrying and creeping from hiding place to hiding place. She'd finished up all of the crisps and they'd been delicious, but salty. She kept on licking around her mouth, catching more little scraps of salt in her whiskers. She stopped every so often where the bank sloped down and she could lean in and slurp a mouthful of river water.

Even when the puppy stopped to drink, she made sure to keep just close enough to follow Avery and the others. Perhaps they had more food? She was still hungry and she didn't know what else to do. There was no sign of her mother anywhere and she'd been searching and calling ever since the people stopped the car and left her here. The puppy was starting to think that she wasn't going to find her mother again.

That girl was the first person who had spoken gently to her in so long. The puppy wasn't sure if she wanted to get any closer to her just yet – but she wasn't going to let the girl out of her sight.

Chapter Four

"You look a bit chirpier than you did this morning," Dad said, giving Avery a little hug as they waited for Mum to find the keys to the cottage.

Avery smiled at him and nodded, but inside she wasn't quite sure what she felt. It had been so exciting to see the puppy again, and Avery had loved watching her gobble up the food – it had almost been like having her own dog, just for a little while. She had hated having to run and catch up with Mum and Dad and Noah.

Avery was just about to tell Dad about the puppy and ask if he thought maybe she was lost, when she caught a tiny glimpse of brown fur under one of the bushes at the side of the garden.

The puppy had followed her!

Avery felt a wild leap of excitement inside.

But what should she do now? It really did seem as though the puppy was lost, that she'd been separated from her owners somehow. Avery had seen her two days running in the same place, and she was really hungry, as though she hadn't eaten for ages. Probably Avery ought to tell Mum and Dad, so they could help find out who she belonged to and get her back to them.

But … Avery didn't want to send the puppy back to her owners.

The tiny dog hadn't been properly looked after, Avery was sure of it. Such a young puppy shouldn't be outside on her own off the lead, should she? But that wasn't even the most important thing. When Avery had got close to the puppy, the little dog had flinched away as though she'd expected something horrible to happen. Thinking about it made Avery feel sick inside. She was sure that someone had frightened the puppy, maybe even hurt her. She couldn't make her go back… Avery bit her lip, thinking about Snowball and

Mum saying that Auntie Meg ought to report her neighbours to the police or the RSPCA. Mum and Dad would say that the puppy *must* go back to her owners, Avery was sure of it...

So she didn't tell Dad about the cute puppy after all. Instead, she deliberately glanced away, so that Dad didn't look where she was looking and spot the little dog. Then she went to help Mum unpack the leftovers from the picnic, and she tucked a couple of sausage rolls into the pocket of her shorts.

"Can I go and read my book in the garden?" Avery asked and Mum nodded.

"Sure. Don't go too close to the river."

Avery hurried out into the garden, hoping that the puppy would be in the same place, looking out at her from under the bush.

"Hey…" she whispered as she came close. "Are you there? I've got more food, look." There was a faint scuffling noise and Avery saw a tiny black nose pop out under the branches. "It's OK," she said. "Here you go." Carefully, she tore the sausage rolls into small pieces and scattered them on the ground.

Then she sat back on her heels, watching eagerly.

After a minute, the puppy wriggled out. She kept on glancing between Avery and the food and back to the bush, as if she was measuring how far she had to go to be safe again. It made Avery feel a bit like crying, watching her. She hopped back a bit to make the puppy feel safer, and watched her hoover up the sausage rolls and then sniff around hopefully for more.

"That was all I could find, sorry," she murmured. The puppy eyed her cautiously, then she padded a little closer and sniffed at Avery's shoes. Avery crouched there, frozen, almost too excited to breathe. Then, very slowly, she stretched out her fingers to the puppy. What would happen? Would the little dog shoot away and her chance be gone? Avery closed her eyes.

There was a moment's pause – she could almost hear the puppy wondering what to do. Then she felt a soft lick against her fingers. Probably she tasted of sausage rolls.

"Hey…" she whispered. She opened her eyes and saw the puppy gazing back at her. She still looked nervous, as though the slightest noise would make her bolt, but she seemed curious too and she stayed put as Avery brushed her fingers along the brown fur on her neck. She even seemed to enjoy it – her thin, whip-like tail thudded happily on the grass.

"You're so pretty," Avery said. The puppy nuzzled against her hand, making her gasp. Was the little dog starting to trust her? "I'm not going to find your owners if they're just going to be horrible to you again," she told the little dog. "You can stay here instead. I can find enough food for you, I know I can." She stroked the puppy's ears lovingly – they were so much softer than the rest of her coat, which was a bit wiry. "I'm going to call you Hazel. Mum says my eyes are hazel and you're the same sort of colour. Light brown with golden bits. It's a nice name. You're Hazel, aren't you?"

The puppy grew used to the garden
over the next couple of days. She found
several good hidey-holes along the
bank of the river and under the bushes.
On the first night,
the girl brought
out a towel
and pushed it
underneath
one of the
bushes to
make a
comfy place
to sleep.
The puppy
still didn't
like sleeping
outdoors much
– there were so

many noises and she could tell that there were other creatures sniffing around, curious about who she was and why she was there. But Avery kept bringing her food and it was much nicer food than she'd been used to before.

There were other people in the garden sometimes and she tried to stay out of their way – she was still nervous. For her, people meant loud, rough voices and slammed doors and food bowls banged down in a hurry. The puppy knew to stay away from people, in case they were angry.

But when Avery came on her own, the puppy would appear at once and they'd hurry down to the river together, so that Avery could bring out whatever she had hidden away in her pockets. It wasn't only the food that the puppy wanted, though. She'd never been fussed and stroked so much, or talked to in the way Avery talked to her, and she was hungry for it. She didn't know what the words meant – though she was starting to recognize that Hazel was a name Avery called her – but it was the way Avery spoke that she loved.

"You're so lovely, Hazel, aren't you?"

"You're such a good dog…"

"Hello, gorgeous Hazel!"

The words were soft and sweet and they made her feel wanted. Sometimes she wished that when Avery disappeared back inside the house, she could go too.

Avery leaned against the willow tree by the edge of the water and patted her knees hopefully. Over the last couple of days, she had stolen every moment she could away from their holiday activities and trips to spend time with the puppy. Hazel had become even more friendly and Avery thought the little puppy might even sit on her lap.

"Come on," she whispered. "You could have a sleep sitting on me. That would be amazing." She sighed. "It can't be a very long sleep though, Hazel. We're going to a museum all about country life later on. Dad says there's going to be sheep shearing and stuff. I'd rather just stay here with you but I can't tell Mum and Dad that. I wish I could tell them about you – but then they'd make me give you back…"

She was silent for a moment, watching Hazel hoover up the last crumbs of the toast she'd saved from breakfast. Then, as the puppy nosed thoughtfully at her legs, Avery whispered, "I'm going to have to tell them something soon, aren't I? Even if you don't go back to your old owner, we can't leave you here on your own when we go home. It's only another week. Maybe you'll have to go to a shelter." She gulped, and then half laughed as Hazel gave a huge sigh and slumped down by her legs, her nose resting gently on Avery's knees. "I wish we could keep you," she said sadly. "But Mum says dogs are hard work – she said that when we saw Freddy, the very first day we were here. I don't think you'd be hard work at all. You could sleep on my bed and I'd take you on loads of walks, even if it was raining, I promise I would."

Avery swallowed hard. "They're going to be so cross with me for keeping you a secret. I'll tell them soon, though. Just a couple more days."

Chapter Five

Avery was eating breakfast several days later when Dad walked in through the back door looking worried. "I've just seen a dog in the garden. Quite a little dog – I think it could be a puppy." He put his coffee mug down on the side and peered out of the window behind the sink. "I tried to catch it but it dashed off – it seemed very nervous."

"Oh dear." Mum got up to look out of the window too. "Do you think it got away from its owners? What should we do?"

"I think I saw a vet's in the village. Maybe they would know if someone had lost their dog."

Avery was sitting at the table, stirring her cereal round and round. Her fingers felt icy with fright. Dad had found Hazel! What was she going to do?

"What sort of dog was it?" she asked, trying not to let her voice shake – it could be another dog, after all... It might be...

"A sweet little brown terrier," Dad said. "I don't think it had a collar, or not that I saw."

"Oh…" Avery whispered. She put her spoon down, twisting her hands in her lap instead. Of course it was Hazel. And she ought to be glad. Now she didn't have to tell Mum and Dad about the puppy – Hazel had done it for her. Avery had told herself that today would have to be the day she said something. It was Wednesday and they were going home on Saturday morning.

"It seems odd for a young dog to be a stray," Mum said. "You wouldn't have thought it would cope on its own, especially not round here with no litter bins to raid or anything like that." She eyed Dad with her head on one side. "You're absolutely sure it wasn't a rabbit?"

Noah snorted with laughter and Dad sighed. "I may not be an expert on dogs, Lara, but I can just about tell the difference between a dog and a rabbit. It was definitely a dog. I'll pop down to the vet's now. There's plenty of time before we set off for that stately home tour."

"Can I come?" Avery asked. They needed to get started looking for Hazel at once, she reckoned. What if Dad had scared her away from the garden entirely? Where would she go? Mum was right. Hazel wouldn't be able to look after herself. Dad hadn't meant to scare her but the puppy was so nervous still, even though she was a lot calmer and happier being around Avery now. She could have raced off anywhere.

"Sure. We can walk into the village. It won't take more than ten minutes."

Avery nodded. She pushed her cereal bowl away – she just couldn't bear to eat anything else. What if they couldn't find Hazel again?

Hazel raced through the bushes, her tail tucked tight against her legs. Who was that man who'd just been in the garden? She'd been looking for Avery

– and breakfast – and she hadn't seen him at first. He'd been sitting on a bench outside the house, sitting very still, and she just hadn't noticed him.

She still remembered the man from her old home when she was back with her mother. He was big and loud and he grabbed at Hazel and her mother and the other puppies, and pushed them around roughly. Hazel had seen him kick her mother once and she remembered her mother's terrified yelp. He hadn't hurt Hazel herself, or not much, but she was terrified of him. The man in the garden had scared her and then he'd wanted to catch her – and Hazel didn't want to be caught. Not by anyone, except maybe Avery. Hazel trusted Avery now. Avery had spent so much time feeding her, and stroking her, and being careful to move gently and speak quietly, and it had worked – she made Hazel feel safe.

The puppy came to the river, nearly plunging into the water in her panic – but then she swerved sideways and began to run along the edge of the water. She needed to get far, far away, and then she was going to hide.

Hazel was tiring now but she kept plodding on by the side of the river as she came up close to the old water mill. She knew this spot, she realized, looking around wearily. This was where Avery had first fed her, where Hazel had licked up all that delicious sweet stuff that Avery had dropped on the path. She remembered how good it had tasted… The puppy hesitated for a moment, wondering where Avery was now – but then there was a sudden burst of noise as a family came along the path from the mill, children racing ahead and their mum calling loudly after them.

Hazel shot away again. She'd never been this far up the river before and it was starting to look very different, narrower and wilder. Hazel didn't know it but she was following one of the streams that led into the river now, a little stream that flowed down from the hillside. The path up the side of the stream was steep and stony, and she was exhausted. At last she stopped and looked back the way she'd come. The hillside seemed completely empty – she heard a bird crying up above her, but that was all.

Wearily, Hazel burrowed underneath a prickly gorse bush covered in sweet-scented yellow flowers. She curled herself into a tiny ball and fell asleep.

Luckily the vet's wasn't too busy and they were able to speak to the veterinary nurse straight away.

"Oh, right." The nurse looked thoughtful as Dad finished explaining. "I don't think anyone's reported a lost dog recently but perhaps she's only just gone missing."

Avery opened her mouth to say that no, the puppy had been around since last week – but then she closed it again hurriedly. She wasn't supposed to know that.

"Can you describe the dog?" the nurse went on.

"Um, well, I didn't see it for that long, but it was small – young looking,

74

a puppy I think. And it was brown
with wiry fur. From the look of it,
I'd say it was a terrier cross, maybe a
Border terrier," Dad said.

Avery darted a sideways glance at
Dad, impressed. She hadn't known
that Hazel might be a Border terrier,
or a terrier cross. She hadn't expected
Dad to know so much about dogs.

"It was a lovely little thing but very
nervous," Dad went on. "It dashed off
as soon as it saw me."

Dad sounded quite sad about it – as though he'd have liked to meet Hazel properly. Just for a moment, Avery wished she'd told Mum and Dad when she first saw the puppy. Perhaps they could all have got to know her. But she supposed Dad would have wanted to report her as missing at once. Hazel would have been whisked away to a shelter, and Avery would never have been able to spend all that time feeding her and loving her. Avery was sure she'd helped make Hazel a lot happier and less nervous than when they'd first met a week ago.

"Well, keep an eye out for her, and let us know if you spot her again," the nurse said, giving Dad a form to write down their contact details. "We'll be in touch with you if anyone tells us about a lost dog – but most owners wouldn't let such a young puppy off the lead. It sounds like she might have been abandoned." She made a face. "People drive out somewhere quiet and just dump unwanted dogs and cats sometimes – it's so sad."

Avery gasped. It was what she'd been thinking, but it was horrible to hear someone actually say it. Dad put his arm round her.

The nurse looked at them apologetically. "I know. I don't understand how people could do something so cruel."

But that was it – there wasn't going to be a search or anything. Avery wasn't sure it had been any use going to the vet's at all. She should have gone straight out into the garden to look for Hazel herself instead. The puppy could be anywhere – and no one was doing anything to find her.

Chapter Six

Back at the cottage, Avery slipped outside into the garden while Mum and Dad looked at the route to get to the stately home that was today's trip out.

"Hazel!" she called quietly, stooping down to peer under the bushes. The puppy might still be there after all... Perhaps she hadn't run very far when

Dad had scared her? But there was no excited scrabbling as Hazel came bounding out to find her.

Avery hurried on down the garden to the river, looking at the reedy clumps along the edge of the water. There was no flash of brown fur there either.

"Please come back…" Avery whispered sadly. "You need us. You need me."

"Avery! Time to go!" Mum was calling from the back door.

Avery trudged slowly up the garden. She really didn't feel like going to see a big old house today. Usually she liked them – there were interesting things to see and sometimes there was a treasure trail or another activity to do. Just not now, when all she could think about was Hazel and whether she'd done the wrong thing not telling Mum and Dad about the puppy to start with.

"What's the matter?" Mum looked at her worriedly as she slumped down in a chair. "You look really upset, Avery. What is it?"

Avery shrugged. Then thinking fast she said, "Actually I don't feel very well. I think going in the car might make it worse too."

"Oh no…" Mum put a hand on her forehead. "You don't seem hot."

"I just feel a bit sick."

"Well, we definitely don't want you going in the car then." Mum sighed. "Oh, that is a pity."

"You could go without me," Avery said suddenly. "I wouldn't mind."

Mum smiled and shook her head. "We can't leave you on your own, sweetie."

"I'll stay with her." Noah looked up. "It's no problem." He smiled hopefully at Mum and she gave him a suspicious look.

"What is this? What's going on with you two? Don't you want to come to Sandings House?"

"Um, not really, Mum…" Noah admitted. "We've been hitting it pretty hard with the trips… The water mill, the country life museum and we've already done at least three stately homes."

"One!" Dad protested. "Only one!"

Noah rolled his eyes. "It felt like more."

"We did the one with all the ghost stories," Avery said, shuddering. "It was really scary."

Mum looked from Noah to Avery and sighed. "I suppose it is quite a lot. Maybe we'll just have a relaxing day here, instead?"

"You really wanted to see the water gardens at the house, though," Dad pointed out. "We could leave Noah and Avery together, couldn't we? Noah's fifteen, after all."

Avery crossed her fingers behind

her back. She was sure Noah wouldn't notice her looking for Hazel. If Mum and Dad let them stay behind, she could go and search for the puppy properly – it was only an hour or so since Dad had spotted her. She couldn't have got that far.

"I suppose…" Mum said doubtfully.

"It'll be fine, Mum. I'll look after Avery. We can make sandwiches for lunch, it's no problem."

"I think I'll just go and lie on my bed and read," Avery said. "Or maybe I'll read in the garden." She still had her fingers crossed in her lap – she hated lying to Mum and Dad, but finding Hazel was more important.

"Mmm. OK." Mum nodded. "We won't be away for too long."

It seemed to take ages for them to get ready to leave. Mum kept fussing about what they ought to have for lunch and then Dad couldn't find where he'd left the car keys. Avery was practically chewing her nails by the time they actually drove away. Then she hurried back into the kitchen, calling to Noah, "I'm going to read by the river, OK?"

Noah eyed her thoughtfully as she opened the back door. "Don't you need a book for that?"

"Oh!" Avery blinked. "Oh… I'll go and get one then." She smiled nervously at him and dashed upstairs to grab her book. She picked up a little packet of cheesy crackers that she'd left over from a picnic too, so she could use them to tempt Hazel back. Over the last few days she'd discovered that Hazel loved anything cheese flavoured.

"You don't look like you're feeling ill," Noah pointed out as she dashed back. "Racing up and down the stairs like that."

Avery shrugged. "Maybe I just didn't want to go to another stately home, like you said." *Why's Noah suddenly being so nosy?* she thought crossly. Usually he didn't pay any attention to what his little sister did. She waved airily at him as she slipped through the door. "See you later!"

She glanced back as she headed down the garden and saw that her brother was watching her out of the window. But he wouldn't be able to see much once she got out by the trees and the river. She hoped not anyway. Avery opened the gate and left her book lying on an old tree stump.

Which way to go? She hovered uncertainly at the edge of the water. *I'll go along the path to the water mill,* she decided. Avery had seen Hazel round there twice, before the puppy followed her back to the cottage. It made sense that she'd run back there. Didn't it?

If there was no sign of Hazel along the path, Avery didn't want to think about what she'd do next.

Hazel lay in the sun next to the gorse bushes, her nose resting on her paws. Her ears kept twitching as shadows of clouds slid past and the wind ruffled her fur. She hadn't seen anything more than a few birds since she'd raced up here along the steep little path between the rocks. Perhaps she shouldn't have come so far. She stood up, looking

uncertainly back down the stony path.
Should she try to go and find Avery?
She was so hungry. Avery had brought
her some food the night
before but she'd had
nothing that
morning.

She sniffed
around
hopefully,
wondering
if perhaps
there would
be something
to eat up here. But
the hillside was bare.
There was only thin, scrubby grass and
stones, and a few little yellow flowers.
Nothing that smelled good to eat.

The puppy whimpered uncertainly, suddenly scared by all the emptiness and quiet up on the hill. She wanted Avery to rub her ears, and whisper to her, and scratch that itchy place just along from her tail. She was on her own again, and she hated it.

Chapter Seven

Avery hurried along the path at the
edge of the river. She was almost at the
water mill now and she hadn't seen any
sign of Hazel. She shivered, wishing
she'd brought her jacket and not just
a thin hoodie. The sun had gone in
and it was definitely getting colder.
She could feel dampness in the air, as
if it was about to rain any minute. She

wrapped her arms around her middle and walked on.

The water mill was set on a smaller stream that fed into the main river – there was a bridge that led over the stream to get to the mill, that was how they'd gone to look at it the other day. But if you didn't cross over the bridge, you kept on going along the side of the narrower stream and up into the hills. It was quiet and more overgrown. Avery hadn't realized that until she got there and she stood, hesitating by the bridge, wondering which way to go. Hazel was twitchy and nervous – she probably wouldn't want to go towards the busy water mill with its café and shop. She was more likely to carry on up the side stream, wasn't she?

Avery looked back the way she'd come, biting her lip. She didn't have a watch on but she'd been walking for a while. Had Noah noticed she wasn't there? Had he maybe even called Mum and Dad by now? Avery shook her head briskly. She didn't want Mum and Dad to be worried but she had to find Hazel. It was her fault that the puppy was out here on her own. If only she'd been sensible and told her parents about Hazel earlier, the puppy would be safe and well looked after by now – even if it wasn't by Avery. She'd put Hazel in danger because she wanted to pretend that the little terrier was hers. Avery sniffed and rubbed the back of her hand across her eyes. It was hard to admit that, but it was true.

She headed on up the path by the narrower stream, walking fast to try and keep warm. It was hard work – the path was getting steeper and wilder now. The stream was tumbling around big rocks,

and there were rocks and small stones all over the path too. It was much harder-going than the flat grassy path by the bigger river.

It was quiet, though, Avery thought. Just the sort of place that a frightened puppy might flee to. It was definitely worth keeping going.

"Hazel!" she called hopefully. "Hazel, come on!"

No answer – just a thin, high bird call. It was so empty up here.

Avery plodded on, looking down at her feet most of the time to make sure she wasn't about to trip on the stones. Then came another bird call, much closer this time, and she straightened up to see what sort of bird it was.

But she couldn't see *anything*.

Avery had felt the damp in the air and noticed the gathering clouds, but now the path was practically blotted out ahead of her – the hillside was wrapped in a swirling white mist.

How could it have come down that suddenly? No wonder she'd been feeling cold. Avery stood on the path, looking around uncertainly. She knew exactly where she was, right by the stream, just like she had been before, but now that everything was grey she felt very small and lost.

"Hazel…" she whispered. She wondered if the puppy was up here in the mist too. Was she scared? Dogs were very good at finding their way around, but Hazel was so little. "Hazel, where are you?" Avery could hear the wobble in her voice. She was getting even colder now she was standing still. She bit her bottom lip – she couldn't just wait here until the mist lifted. She had no idea how long that would take, it could be hours. She had to go on up and keep trying to find Hazel, or follow the stream back down the hill. It seemed more dangerous to keep going, when she couldn't see and she didn't know what was ahead of her. There could be a cliff or something – she had no idea. If she went back she could tell Mum and Dad, like she should have done days ago, and they could all come back and search for Hazel together. Even if it did mean that Hazel had to go to a shelter.

Sadly, Avery turned round and started to pick her way back down the path, hoping that soon the mist would lift. It was spooky, hardly being able to see her hand in front of her face. She kept thinking about that house they'd visited, with its gallery full of pictures and stories of ghosts – there had even been films of people talking about the ghosts they'd seen, ghosts and other strange creatures. All of them round here too. Apparently there were all sorts of dark fairies and elves that liked to tempt people away from paths and lose them in the hills. Avery shuddered. The stories had seemed spooky and a bit funny in a nice warm house. Now they felt horribly real.

She kept on calling for Hazel every couple of minutes, but the mist seemed to swallow up all the noise, as if she was wrapped in a grey blanket. It made it hard to hear the noise of the stream on the rocks too – she couldn't tell where the bank was at all now.

Avery stopped, her heart suddenly thumping. The stream had been right next to her, she knew it had, but the noise had disappeared completely. She took a couple of steps sideways, very cautiously, so she didn't fall in.

There was no stream.

She had wandered off the path in the mist. She was lost.

Distracted and panicky, Avery ran

a few steps forwards, still searching for the stream – for anything that she could see! Then she felt her foot slide out from under her – so quickly that she hardly understood what was happening – and she was sprawled on the ground, her foot twisted painfully underneath her.

Avery yelled out loud, half from fright and half from the pain in her ankle. She leaned over, gasping and sobbing, cradling her foot. It hurt too much to think of moving just yet.

After a few minutes, she managed to gulp down her tears a little and try to move her foot. She could wiggle it, just about, even though it hurt. Wincing, she ran her fingers down her ankle – it didn't seem to be at a funny angle, although it was already starting to swell up a bit. Hopefully she'd just twisted it… But there was no way she was going to be able to walk with her ankle like this.

She was stuck.

Further round the hill, Hazel sat up,
her ears sharply pricked. She had
heard something – a person. She
had been curled up at the edge of
the gorse patch, nervously eyeing the
mist. She didn't really understand
what it was, but she knew she didn't
like it. It was damp and chilly and
she couldn't see. She turned slowly,
her ears twitching and swivelling,
listening intently. It was hard with
all this strange grey stuff – it muffled
the sounds… But yes, there! She
could hear more noises, something
that sounded quite like a whimpering
puppy.

Hazel looked doubtfully at the mist.

The gorse bushes were cold and not that comfortable, but at least they felt fairly safe. Did she really want to go out into it?

The noises, though… There was something about them that tugged inside her and made her want to find out what was wrong. With a huffy little sigh, Hazel set out across the side of the hill, following those sad, frightened sounds.

She'd been trotting along for a few minutes when she caught a scent too – one that she recognized.
Avery was here! Avery had come to find her!

Hazel whined excitedly and sped up, darting through the mist and sniffing eagerly at the trail.

Avery tensed up, terrified. There was a scratching, pattering noise now – not the stream, but something moving towards her. An animal, or maybe … something else… She thought of all those eerie stories about fairies again and tried not to scream. If she was quiet, perhaps it would go past her?

Then something warm and round and furry flung itself at her, landing heavily in her lap. Avery squeaked – and then found that the furry thing was licking her chin, her face, all over her. Licking and yelping and squirming as if it was too excited to keep still.

"Hazel?" she whispered delightedly, almost forgetting the pain in her ankle.

"You found me! Oh, Hazel, I was supposed to be coming to rescue you!"

Hazel curled up in Avery's lap for a few moments, letting Avery fuss over her. It was amazing how much less scary the misty hillside felt with a warm little dog to hold. But then Avery felt her wriggle away. The puppy stood next to her, looking hopefully back down the hill.

"Oh!" Avery looked around. "It's going! Look, Hazel, I can see you!" The mist was shredding away into wisps and Avery could see piled rocks further across the hillside that looked like they might show the path of the stream. She hadn't wandered that far after all. If she could get back over there, she'd know how to head home.

She put her hands flat on the grass and carefully tried to lever herself upright. But as soon as she put any weight on her left ankle, she collapsed back down with a gasp. It *really* hurt. Perhaps she could walk on it if she had a crutch, or even just a stick to lean on, but there was nothing like that here.

Hazel was watching her, head tipped sideways as if she was confused. She whined, scratching at the grass with one front paw.

"You think I should just get up and follow you, don't you?" Avery sighed. "I can't,

108

Hazel. I wish I could. Hazel! Hey! Where are you going?" Avery felt her voice rise in panic. Hazel had darted away between the rags of mist, making for those rocks by the stream. Avery could hardly see her.

"Please don't go!" she called, hearing the frightened shake in her voice.

But Hazel had disappeared already, leaving Avery alone on the empty hillside.

Chapter Eight

Hazel hesitated outside the back door to the cottage. She could hear raised voices inside and they made her nervous.

This morning she had run all that way up into the hills to get away from the tall man with the deep voice. Now she was going to show herself to him on purpose. It seemed wrong – but she had to do it. She didn't really understand why Avery hadn't followed her back down the path but she could tell that something wasn't right. Avery had been making those hurt noises and she didn't seem to be able to move. All Hazel could think to do was find the people at the cottage and get them to help.

Slowly, cautiously, she lifted one front paw and scratched at the door. Then again, louder. She waited, listening to the voices die away inside the cottage and then footsteps approaching the door. She cringed on the doorstep, forcing herself to stay when all she wanted to do was run.

The door opened and she looked up to find the boy she'd often seen with Avery staring down at her.

"Dad, is this the dog you saw?"

Hazel pressed herself flat against the step as the tall man appeared next to the boy. "Yes! Oh… Is she scared of me?"

"Looks like it," the boy said worriedly. "Um. Maybe you should crouch down? When Liam's family got a dog from a shelter, she was terrified of tall men. Liam was always having to pick her up if they walked past somebody tall. Maybe it's the same thing."

The tall man squatted down in the doorway and spoke gently to Hazel.

"It's OK. Don't be scared."

Hazel twitched her tail very, very slightly. The man was big, but now he sounded gentle, like Avery. She watched warily as a woman appeared at the door too. "Is this the puppy you saw this morning, Sam? Look, she's very sweet, but right now we need to work out where Avery's gone. Noah, do you really not know when she left?"

"I told you," the boy muttered. "I didn't notice. It can't have been that long…"

"You were supposed to be looking after her!"

"I said I was sorry… But Mum, don't you think it's a bit weird that this dog's here again? Do you think Avery knew about it? All that time she spent down by the river. And I'm sure I saw her hiding bits of food in her pockets, as if she was saving it for someone else."

"She did keep disappearing out into the garden," the woman said slowly. "I thought she just liked being by the water…"

"Why would she keep the dog a secret?" The tall man glanced up, frowning.

The boy shrugged. "I don't know. But she loves dogs, Dad. I can just see her deciding to rescue a puppy. Maybe she thought you wouldn't let her do it if she told you."

Hazel watched uncertainly as the three of them talked – she had seen them all with Avery. These were the people she needed. Avery needed them.

She hopped off the step and turned towards the river, gazing back at them hopefully. Then she gave a little bark.

They only stared at her. Why weren't they coming? Hazel barked again.

"I told you!" the boy stepped out into the garden. "She definitely wants us to follow her."

"You've watched too many films," the tall man said, shaking his head. "Then again, Avery really wanted to come to the vet's, didn't she? She seemed pretty worried about the dog." He followed the boy, his steps slow and uncertain, and Hazel's tail wagged faster. She ran a little way and then doubled back with some encouraging yaps.

"You know, I think Noah's right," the woman said. "Look at her. She's practically rounding us up like a sheepdog."

"You don't think we should be calling the police about Avery?" the tall man asked. "This feels like a bit of a wild goose chase." He stopped for a moment and Hazel raced back to stand in front of him and bark, right there, right by his feet. He had to hurry up! She could still hear that frightened note in Avery's voice. She needed to get Avery's people to her now.

"All right," the man muttered. "She's definitely trying to tell us something."

Hazel raced down the garden to the riverbank and then led the family along the path. She kept stopping to check that they were following her but they stayed close behind.

"Up here?" the woman murmured
as she headed on to the path by the
side of the stream. "This leads up into
the hills. Avery wouldn't come all this
way, would she?"

"She would if she was looking for
the dog," Noah said slowly. "Dad, you
scared the dog away this morning, didn't
you? I reckon Avery went after her. She
was definitely jumpy when you left to go
to that house. She said she was going to
read in the garden, but she hadn't even

remembered to bring a book. That was just an excuse, I'm sure of it. We've got to keep following this puppy."

Hazel yapped, circling around the boy's feet to try and get him to stop talking and hurry up. Then she darted out in front of them again, scurrying along the stony path to lead them to Avery.

Up on the hill, Avery was sitting with her arms wrapped tightly around her knees, trying to stop her teeth from chattering.

How was it so cold? It was meant to be summer! She felt shivery and strange and her ankle wasn't starting to feel better at all. In fact, it was feeling worse and worse.

I wish Hazel had stayed with me, she thought miserably. *I hope she's OK. I hope she's not too scared, all on her own…*

The last wisps of mist were clearing away completely now and Avery could see quite a long way down the hill. She peered forwards, blinking hard – was that something moving far away on the path? It looked like people! They'd help her get down, wouldn't they? Or at least call Mum and Dad for her. She knew Mum's number off by heart.

The people coming up the path had

a little dog with them and Avery's heart jumped inside her, thinking of Hazel. She sat up a little straighter and waved, hoping that they'd see her. The dog raced on up the path ahead of them and Avery smiled sadly. She looked so like Hazel. Perhaps it was because Avery couldn't stop thinking about her.

It took a couple more seconds for her to realize – the dog didn't just look like Hazel. It *was* Hazel – Hazel and Mum and Dad and Noah, all hurrying up the path towards her.

And then Hazel was right there with her, barking and bouncing and trying to lick her ears – until Dad got there to pick Avery up and hug her and carry her back down the hill.

"If she does have a microchip, does
that mean we have to give her back?"
Avery whispered to Mum. She had
Mum's hand in hers and she was
squeezing it very tight. Noah was
gently holding on to Hazel while the
vet examined her. Avery had wanted
to do it but she was still having a hard

time standing up for long. Mum and Dad had taken her to A&E, and her ankle was only sprained, but now it was a few hours after she'd fallen and it had swollen up like a balloon.

It really hurt too – the only good thing was it meant Mum and Dad were more worried about her than cross. Mum kept on saying things like "Why didn't you just tell us?" and "I can't believe you kept her a secret all this time!"

Avery had tried to explain why but it all came out jumbled – how scared Hazel was, and how angry Mum had been about Auntie Meg and Snowball and the neighbours... She still wasn't sure that Mum and Dad really understood. But Hazel had found Avery for them, after they'd been so worried. Avery had a feeling that they'd do anything for the brave little puppy now.

Hazel was hunched over on the vet's table and she looked desperately scared. But she hadn't growled or tried to bite – Avery felt so proud of her.

"I don't know," Mum said. "Not if they weren't looking after her, surely?"

"She looks quite healthy," the vet said, looking up. "Just a little thin. Such a good girl. OK, let's scan her."

Avery nodded, swallowing hard.

The vet picked up something that looked a bit like the scanner at the supermarket and held it near Hazel's neck. "No … she hasn't got one. Definitely no chip." She smiled at

Avery. "So … she could go home with you. We've even got a spare dog carrier we can let you have for the car."

Avery stood up and limped to the table, and Hazel crawled over to lean against her. Avery smiled as she felt Hazel's nose squished into her T-shirt, and then she looked pleadingly at Mum and Dad. "I know you said having a dog was a lot of work but I promise I'll look after her. My ankle's going to get better soon and then I'll do all the walks, I really will."

"I think she belongs with us now," Mum said. "She rescued you. I hate to think how long you could have been alone on that hill if she hadn't come to find us. She's so clever."

"Dad?" Avery asked hopefully. "I

know she thinks you're a bit scary…"

"She's great, Dad," Noah put in. "She just needs a good family to look after her and she won't be so frightened."

Dad held out his hand and let Hazel sniff it cautiously. Then she licked him, just once, very fast, and Dad grinned. "Definitely getting more friendly." He nodded. "Like your mum said, Avery, we can't give her up now. Let's take her back to the cottage."

"Did you hear that?" Avery whispered, leaning down close to Hazel's gingery velvet ears. "We're taking you home."

Avery wasn't sure if Hazel knew what the word meant – maybe she heard something in her voice – but the little dog leaned even closer. Her tail started to swish from side to side, sweeping across the table, and Avery was sure that somehow, she understood.

HOLLY
WEBB

Holly Webb started out as a children's
book editor and wrote her first series for
the publisher she worked for. She has been
writing ever since, with over one hundred
books to her name. Holly lives in Berkshire,
with her husband and three children.
Holly's pet cats are always nosying around
when she is trying to type on her laptop.

For more information
about Holly Webb visit:

www.holly-webb.com